Nighttime™
Too Dark to See

Nighttime™
Too Dark to See

by Todd Strasser

Scholastic Inc.

New York Toronto London Auckland Sydney
Mexico City New Delhi Hong Kong Buenos Aires

For Gina and Matt with thanks.
T. S.

ISBN-13: 978-0-439-80068-6
ISBN-10: 0-439-80068-4

12 11 10 9 8 7 6 5 4 3 2 1   8 9 10 11 12 13/0

Printed in the U.S.A.
First printing, February 2008

CONTENTS

The Thing Under the Bed

"What are you doing?" Justin Porter asked his little sister, Amanda. Justin was eleven years old. He was in the hallway outside Amanda's room. Amanda was seven. She was standing on the chair next to her bed. Amanda was wearing her pink pajama bottoms and a pink T-shirt. She was holding her white unicorn and her tattered old "banky" in her arms. Her "banky" was all that was left of her favorite pink baby blanket.

"I'm getting into bed," said Amanda.

"If you're getting into bed, why are you standing on that chair?" Justin asked.

"Because," said Amanda.

"Because what?" said Justin.

"Go away," said Amanda.

"Because you're going to jump from that chair to your bed," Justin said. "Because you're afraid."

Amanda scrunched her face up like she was going to cry. It was true that she was afraid. Her bed had long legs, and there was a big space under it. She was afraid that if she stood too close to the space, something would reach out and grab her. So every night, she gathered her unicorn and "banky" in her arms and climbed up on the chair beside the bed. Then, holding those things very tightly, she jumped from the chair to the bed.

"There's nothing to be afraid of," Justin said. "There's nothing under your bed."

Amanda didn't move from the chair. As long as her brother was there, she wouldn't jump to the bed. "Go away," she said, trying her best not to cry.

But Justin didn't go away. He went over to the

bed and got down on his hands and knees. "Hey, Thing Under the Bed," he said. "Come out, come out wherever you are."

Amanda held her breath. Her heart raced. She knew the thing under the bed was there. Sometimes, at night, she heard it breathing.

"Come on, Thing Under the Bed," Justin said. "If you're here, show yourself."

A moment later, he backed away from the bed. "See? There's nothing there. If there was, it would have gotten me by now."

"Mom!" Amanda cried.

"Scaredy-cat," Justin snarled, and backed out of the room.

A moment later, Mrs. Porter arrived. "What's wrong, hon?"

"Justin's teasing me!" Amanda said.

Mrs. Porter looked in Justin's room. Amanda's brother was sitting on the floor, pretending to play with his Legos.

"Don't tease your sister, Justin," his mother said.

While her mother's back was turned, Amanda jumped from the chair to the bed. Then she crawled under the covers and clutched her unicorn and "banky" tight. Mrs. Porter came into the room and tucked her in. She kissed Amanda on the forehead and whispered, "When I was your age, I was afraid, too."

Mrs. Porter left the door open and the hall light on and went into her room. Amanda lay very still and listened. She wasn't sure, but she thought she heard the thing under the bed rustle. But she knew that as long as she was under the covers she was safe. Soon she fell asleep.

The next evening, just before Amanda's bedtime, Justin crawled under her bed. He crawled to the very far corner and curled up so that his sister wouldn't see him. Then he waited.

A little while later, he saw his sister's feet come into the room. He heard the chair squeak as she climbed up on it. He heard the soft *thump!* when she jumped from the chair to the bed. The bedcovers rustled as she snuggled under them.

A few moments later, Mrs. Porter came to tuck in her daughter.

Justin waited until his mother turned off the

bedroom light and left the room. Then he started to breathe loudly. He scraped his fingers against the carpet under the bed like a monster with claws. He made a deep monster groan.

"Mommy!" In the bed above him, Amanda shrieked with fear. *Thump!* Her feet hit the floor, and she ran as fast as she could out of the room.

Justin grinned. All he had to do now was get out from under the bed and back into his room. He'd pretend to be playing with his Legos. He'd pretend he knew nothing about what had happened in his sister's room.

He started to crawl.

His fingers scraped against the carpet under the bed.

But he didn't move.

He couldn't get out from under the bed.

Something was holding him from behind.

The Open Door

Tara Richards was in bed. The small green night-light by the door glowed. The radiator gurgled and hissed. She yawned. Both of her parents had already come in to say good night. Tara's eyes were growing heavy. She rolled over and felt her head sink into the pillow. She was just about to close her eyes when she noticed that the closet door was opened a little bit.

Tara sat up and hugged her teddy. "Mom! Dad!" she called.

"What is it, Tara?" her mother answered from her bedroom.

"My closet's open," Tara called back.

"Just close it, hon," called her father.

"I can't," Tara called back. "I'm scared."

Tara heard her mother whisper and her father mutter. The springs of her parents' bed squeaked. A moment later, her father appeared in her doorway. "Suppose I stand here and watch while you close the closet?" he said.

Tara clutched her teddy and shook her head. "It's scary."

"You can't expect us to come in and close your closet door every time you leave it open," her father said.

Tara knew that her father was annoyed. "It's just at night," she said.

"You can't expect us to come in every night," said her father.

Mrs. Richards joined her husband in the

doorway. "What's wrong? Why haven't you come back to bed?"

"I'm trying to explain to Tara that she can't expect us to come in every night and close her closet door for her," said Mr. Richards.

"Is it really such a big deal?" Mrs. Richards asked her husband.

"No, but it's silly," said Mr. Richards. "There's nothing in her closet. And there's no reason she can't close it herself."

"There *could* be something in there," said Tara.

"You're getting too old for that," said her father.

"I don't think that's fair," Tara's mother said to her husband. "I can't go to sleep unless all the closet doors in our room are closed."

"You're too old for that, too," Mr. Richards told his wife.

"Then why do you make sure all the downstairs doors are locked every night?" Mrs. Richards asked her husband.

"That's different," said Tara's father. "Someone could come in."

"Who?" asked his wife. "We live way out in the country. Our nearest neighbor is half a mile away."

"Doesn't matter," said Mr. Richards.

"And what about the garage door?" asked Mrs. Richards.

"Someone might take something," said her husband.

"If you can't go to bed without being sure all those doors are closed, then you should understand why Tara can't go to bed unless her closet door is closed," said Mrs. Richards. Then she stepped into Tara's room and closed the closet door tightly.

The next morning, Tara woke early. Her room was filled with sunlight. Tara stretched and yawned. She turned her head.

Her closet door was open.

Tara caught her breath and tensed. Suddenly, she felt fully awake. Clutching her teddy, she slid out of bed and quickly inched across the room, never taking her eyes off the open closet door. When she reached the room doorway, she sprinted into her parents' room.

Her parents were still asleep. Tara crawled over

the bed and got under the covers with them. They both woke up.

"What are you doing?" her mother asked with a yawn.

Tara told her about the closet door being open.

Mr. Richards turned to his wife. "I thought you closed it last night."

"I did." Mrs. Richards yawned and stretched. "It must have popped open on its own."

"It never did that before," Tara said.

"Don't worry." Mrs. Richards put her arms around Tara and hugged her.

But then Tara felt her mother's arms stiffen.

"Why is *our* closet open?" Mrs. Richards asked. Tara could hear the alarm in her mother's voice.

Tara and her father sat up in bed. Across the room, the double doors of her parents' closet were wide open.

"I guess you forgot to close them," said Mr. Richards.

"I didn't forget," Tara's mother said firmly. "I closed those doors last night. Just like I do every night."

"Are you *certain?*" Mr. Richards asked.

"Yes," said Mrs. Richards.

"Then I guess the monster in the closet opened them," said Tara's father.

"Mom!" Tara gasped fearfully and hugged her mother.

"That's not funny," Mrs. Richards scolded her husband. Then she stroked Tara's head. "Don't be afraid. There are no monsters in our closets."

"Then why was mine open this morning?" Tara asked. "And why is yours open?"

Mrs. Richards looked at her husband.

"Don't ask me," said Mr. Richards.

"It doesn't bother you?" Mrs. Richards asked her husband.

"Not at all," said Tara's father.

"How do you explain that *both* closets are open?" Tara's mother asked.

"I can't," answered her husband. "But the one thing I do know is that no one snuck into our house last night while we were asleep and opened them."

"How do you know?" asked Tara.

"Because I know I locked all the downstairs doors last night," said Mr. Richards. "No one could have come in."

"Are you *certain*?" asked his wife.

"Yes," said her husband.

Just then, they all heard a creak from downstairs. Tara's parents shared a look.

"That sounded like a door," said Mrs. Richards.

Mr. Richards frowned and got out of bed. He pulled on his robe and went out into the upstairs hallway. The air in the hallway felt colder than usual. Mr. Richards wondered if the heat had gone off during the night.

He started down the stairs but stopped halfway.

The front door was wide open.

Cold air was blowing in.

Mr. Richards felt a chill.

He was certain he'd locked that door the night before.

The Silver Ghost

Each summer, Alex Crane and his mom went to visit their cousins in the country. Alex always looked forward to the visit because he got to spend time with his cousin David. Together they would play ball and hunt frogs and climb trees.

"Can Alex and I stay out after dark tonight?" David asked his parents at dinner on the first night Alex and his mom were there. "We want to go owl hunting."

"Oh, no," Mrs. Crane said quickly. "I don't want you wandering around in the woods at night with guns. That sounds dangerous."

"We're not going to hunt them with guns," David said. "We're just going to look for them."

"It's really not dangerous," added David's father. "This isn't the city. Out here in the country nothing bad ever happens."

"They could fall in the dark and hurt themselves," Alex's mother said.

David's father turned to the boys. "You boys promise to take flashlights and stay together, right?"

"We will!" Alex and David said.

As soon as dinner was over, David and Alex each took a flashlight and went out into the dark. Above them, the stars twinkled and the moon glowed. Alex felt nervous. In the city, he was never allowed to go out after dark. In the city, bad things happened all the time.

"Let's go this way," said David. He led Alex across his backyard and through the tall grass beyond that. They came to a steep gravel slope. At the bottom were train tracks. David started to scramble down the slope.

"Are you sure this is safe?" Alex asked. "What if a train comes?"

"Don't worry," David said. "These tracks haven't been used in years."

Alex shined his flashlight at the tracks. They did look old and brown with rust. Tall green weeds grew between the railroad ties. He went down the slope and joined David at the bottom.

He and David walked along the tracks. They aimed their flashlights down at the old wooden railroad ties so that they didn't trip. Soon the tracks entered some dark woods. Tall shadowy trees rose up on both sides of them. Alex felt nervous. The woods looked scary. Alex knew the train tracks were supposed to be abandoned. But what if a train did come and they had to run into those woods? Even with a flashlight, Alex didn't feel safe.

"Listen real carefully," David whispered. "This is where the owls are."

Alex listened. He heard the rustle of the leaves

in the trees. Then, from the distance came a faint sound that scared him. "It's a train!" He gasped.

"No, silly, that's an owl," said David.

"But it sounded like the toot of a train whistle," said Alex.

"Not a toot," said David. "A hoot. You'd know it if you'd heard an owl before."

It was true that Alex had never heard an owl hoot before.

David aimed his flashlight toward the dark trees beside the railroad tracks. "Let's go," he said.

"Into the woods?" Alex swallowed nervously.

"You want to see the owl, don't you?" David asked.

Alex wasn't sure he wanted to see the owl enough to go into those woods. David seemed to understand. "Okay, you wait here. I'll go look for the owl. If I find it, I'll come back and get you."

"But your father said we should stay together," Alex said.

"I've been in the woods alone lots of times," David said. "It's no big deal. Just wait here. If I find that owl, I'll come right back and get you."

Before Alex could argue, David disappeared into the dark woods.

Alex stood on the tracks and waited. He looked up at the twinkling stars and the round glowing moon. He looked at the dark woods. He waited. And waited. He wondered what he would do if David didn't come back. He wondered what he would do if a train came.

Then he heard that sound again. This time, it was a little bit louder and sounded a little bit closer. David may have said that it was an owl, but it still sounded like a train to Alex. He looked down the tracks in one direction, and then the other. About a hundred yards away was a small, dark building. Alex was surprised that he hadn't noticed it before. Suddenly, through a window, a faint dot of yellow light glowed as if someone was lighting something.

Alex walked closer. Through the window, he thought he saw a small reddish glow inside. He walked closer. Now he could smell the sweet scent of burning pipe tobacco.

Alex walked closer. Now he could see the outline

of someone sitting in the building. It was an old man with a train engineer's cap. He was smoking a pipe. Each time he puffed, the pipe glowed red.

Alex stepped closer. Suddenly, the man turned and looked at him through the window. Frightened, Alex jumped back. Through the window, he saw the man rise. Alex backed away farther. The man with the pipe stepped out onto the porch next to the tracks. Alex felt his stomach begin to knot from nervousness.

The old man took the pipe from his mouth and said, "Howdy."

"Uh, hi," Alex said.

"Nice night, huh?" said the man.

Alex swallowed. "I guess."

Suddenly, he heard the train whistle sound in the distance. Alex twisted around to look. This time, he was sure it was a train whistle and not an owl. The man reached into his pocket and took out a watch. "The Silver Ghost, right on time."

"A train?" Alex said.

The old man smiled. "Can't be nothin' else. I'd get off those tracks if I was you."

Alex jumped away from the tracks. He stood in a small clearing between the tracks and the dark woods. The train's whistle sounded again, and now Alex could see a glowing yellow light in the distance.

As he watched, the light grew brighter. Soon Alex could hear the chugging of the train's engine and feel the vibrations through the ground under his feet.

Toot! Tooooooooooot! The train's whistle blew. With a loud rumble, it roared past. Alex felt the wind in his face. The branches above him swayed and the leaves rustled. He could smell the oil and diesel fuel. The ground under his feet trembled. He stepped back even farther.

The train passed. The leaves continued to rustle, and the weeds and tall grass beside the tracks swayed. The wind quickly eased, and the roar grew dim.

Down the tracks, Alex saw a flashlight beam come out of the woods. It was David. Alex ran toward him. "Did you see it?"

David shook his head. "I looked all over. I heard it, but I couldn't see it."

"Not the owl," Alex said. "The train."

David made a face. "What train?"

"The Silver Ghost. It just came by— just before you came out of the woods. You had to have seen it. And even if you didn't, you would have heard it."

"I didn't hear anything," David said. "I told you these tracks are abandoned."

"No, they're not," Alex insisted. "The Silver Ghost just came by. I mean, it must have been going a hundred miles per hour!"

David shook his head. "Why do you think it was called the Silver Ghost?"

"Because the old man said so," Alex said.

"What old man?"

"The one with the pipe." Alex turned and pointed at the dark building.

But there was no building there.

And no old man.

Alex took a deep sniff. The smell of pipe tobacco was still in the air. He was about to ask David if he smelled it. But then he changed his mind. No matter what he said, David would never believe him.

What's Behind You?

It was Mother's Day, and Mr. Hill surprised his wife with a big arrangement of flowers. In the kitchen, young Katie Hill helped her mother put the flowers in a glass vase. There were so many flowers that the vase had to be perfectly balanced or it would fall over.

"Maybe we should divide the flowers into two vases," Mrs. Hill said. "Then it won't tip so easily."

"But they look so nice when they're all together," Katie said.

"I guess you're right," said her mother. "We'll just be careful."

When they were finished, they put the vase of flowers in the middle of the kitchen table.

Later that night, Mr. Hill tucked Katie into bed.

"Good night, Daddy," Katie said. "Those flowers were really pretty. Mom loves them."

"I'm glad," her father said. "Now good night, Katie. Sleep tight. Don't let the bedbugs bite."

"I won't, Daddy," Katie said with a yawn.

Mr. Hill went to the door and turned out the bedroom light. "See you in the morning."

Katie closed her eyes and went to sleep. She was the youngest in her family, and each evening she went to bed first. The rest of her family would go to sleep later. They all thought that Katie— like most little girls— stayed in bed and slept all night.

But Katie Hill had a secret. Almost every night, she got out of bed and went downstairs to the kitchen for a snack. It was always very late, long after the rest of her family had gone to sleep. The house was always dark and quiet. Katie was always scared. But as long as she had Midnight with her, she felt safe.

Midnight was the Hills' Labrador retriever. He was jet-black from the tip of his nose to the tip of his tail. Even his nails were black. In the dark, he was almost invisible. Every night, Midnight slept on the floor beside Katie's bed. He did not come into her room until everyone else had gone to sleep.

And every night when Katie went downstairs for her snack, Midnight followed her.

That night, after she fell asleep, Katie had a bad dream. She dreamed that her older brother, Tom, and Midnight were roughhousing in the kitchen. There was a crash when Tom accidentally knocked over the vase of Mother's Day flowers. The vase crashed to the floor and shattered, sending sharp shards of glass everywhere. Midnight stepped on a shard and howled in pain. The broken glass went deep into his paw.

Katie woke. She was breathing hard and felt frightened. She loved Midnight very much and didn't want anything bad to happen to him. She lay in the dark and listened. The house was quiet and still. She could hear the dog breathing on the floor beside her bed. Katie reached over the side of her bed. She touched the dog's fur and felt his ribs rise and fall as he slept.

Katie felt a wave of relief. It was only a dream. Everything was okay. She went back to sleep.

A little while later, Katie woke again. Now she was hungry. It was time for her nightly visit to the kitchen.

She slipped out of bed and walked quietly across the room. Behind her the dog rose and followed. Katie went down the stairs. The steady breaths behind her made her feel safe. She always wanted Midnight to stay behind her. She could rely on her own eyes to see what was ahead of her, but not what was behind. That was Midnight's job.

Downstairs, they walked through the shadows toward the kitchen. When they crossed the dining room, Katie heard the click of dog nails on the floor behind her.

They entered the kitchen. Something seemed different, but in the dark Katie wasn't sure what it was. And she never turned on the lights, for fear of waking her family.

Katie opened the pantry. Just as she did every night, she took out three chocolate chip cookies. While she stood at the counter eating a cookie with her right hand, she took another cookie in her left hand and held it down for Midnight. Katie felt the dog take the cookie out of her hand. She felt the hardness of his teeth and the wetness of his tongue on her fingers.

Katie ate her second cookie and left the kitchen. Once again, she heard the click of nails on the floor as she went through the dining room. She heard the dog pant lightly as they climbed back up the stairs. In her room, she got back into bed. She reached down and patted the dog gently, then went to sleep.

In the morning when Katie woke up, Midnight wasn't on the floor beside her bed. Katie wasn't surprised. The dog often rose early and went downstairs to be let out. Katie got out of bed and went down. In the kitchen, Mr. and Mrs. Hill were sitting quietly at the table. Now Katie realized what had been different when she entered the kitchen the night before.

"Where are the flowers?" she asked.

"Tom and Midnight were running around last night, and they accidentally knocked over the vase," Mrs. Hill said.

Katie looked around. "Where's Tom, anyway? And where's Midnight?"

"Tom's still sleeping," Mr. Hill said. "And Midnight is at the twenty-four-hour emergency vet. When the vase broke, he cut his paw very badly."

Katie was confused. "This morning?"

"No, last night," said Mrs. Hill. "Just after you went to sleep. The vet wanted to keep Midnight overnight to make sure he'd be okay."

"But Midnight was here last night," said Katie.

"No, honey, he was at the vet," said Mrs. Hill.

"That can't be," said Katie.

"Why not?" asked Mr. Hill.

Katie didn't answer. She felt a shiver and stared down at her hand. If Midnight hadn't eaten out of it last night, then what had?

Game Boy

Peter Lenox played so many videogames that his friends called him Game Boy. Peter played his PSP at the kitchen table when he ate breakfast. Then he played it while he walked to the bus stop. He played it while he waited for the bus, and he played it while he rode on the bus.

Everyone knew that you got in trouble if you were caught by a teacher playing videogames at school. But sometimes Peter couldn't resist. At least once a week, a teacher would catch Peter playing his PSP and take it away. Peter would have to wait until after school to get it back. That meant missing the bus home. But Peter didn't care. He just walked home playing the PSP.

Each day when Peter got home, he stopped playing videogames just long enough to do his homework and his chores. He stopped just long enough to eat dinner and practice violin for twenty minutes. He stopped and read ten pages in a book. But he spent every other waking second playing.

Peter's parents didn't know what to do. Peter got good grades in school. He was a well-behaved and obedient boy. If Mrs. Lenox asked him to help with the dishes after dinner, he would always help. And then he would go play videogames. If Mr. Lenox asked him to take out the garbage, Peter would do it right away, and then play videogames.

Mr. and Mrs. Lenox got tired of trying to think of ways to keep their son from playing videogames every second of the day. Sometimes it was easier to let him play. But it still bothered them very much.

"Isn't there anything else you want to do?" Mrs. Lenox asked.

Peter shook his head. He stared at the screen of his PSP. His thumbs moved so fast they were a blur.

"Is there anything we can do to get you to turn that thing off?" Mr. Lenox asked.

"Why?" Peter asked, without looking up.

"Because playing videogames all the time can't be good for you," said his father.

"Why not?" asked Peter.

"Because it can't be," Mr. Lenox said.

"But I get good grades in school and practice violin every night and do all the chores you ask me to do," Peter said.

"You could spend more time outside," said Mrs. Lenox.

"I have allergies," said Peter.

This was true. Whenever Peter went outside, his eyes began to itch and swell. His nose began to run, and he would sneeze and cough.

"You could spend more time with your friends," said Mr. Lenox.

"They're always busy," Peter said.

This was also true. Peter's friends played sports. They took lessons and went to tutors. They participated in after school activities. They did homework and practiced their instruments. Some of Peter's friends even avoided him because all he wanted to do was play videogames.

Peter's parents pursed their lips in frustration.

"What's wrong with playing videogames?" Peter asked.

"There's nothing wrong with it as long as it's not the only thing you do," said his father.

"We're just worried that if you play so much you might someday *become* a videogame," said his mother.

Peter gave her a puzzled look.

"Well, not really," Mrs. Lenox said. "But you know what I mean."

The truth was that Peter didn't know what she meant. But it didn't matter. He liked playing videogames, and they didn't hurt anyone.

So Peter played more and more. He didn't notice when his friends spent less time with him. He didn't realize that he didn't talk to people as much as he used to. He wasn't aware that even when he wasn't playing videogames, the game music still played in his head.

Sometimes he even pretended to be the characters in the games.

Sometimes he didn't even need his PSP. He could play a game in his head without it.

At night after the lights went out, he played his PSP under the covers.

His dreams were videogame dreams.

Peter dreamed he was in a videogame. He was playing against the other characters. The videogame music was all around him.

"Peter?" It was his father's voice.

Peter stopped playing and looked around. Through a small video screen, he could see his bedroom. The room was filled with sunlight. The clock beside his bed said 8:37. Peter knew it had to be morning.

"Peter?" On the screen, Peter saw his father step into the bedroom and look around with a puzzled expression.

"Is he there?" Peter heard his mother ask.

On the screen, Peter saw his father shake his head and answer, "No."

Now his mother entered the bedroom. "That's strange," she said with a frown. "Where could he be?"

"Did you check the bathroom?" Peter's father asked.

"Yes," said his mother. "He's not there."

Through the video screen, Peter watched as his father came closer. "He couldn't have gone far because he left his game."

Peter's mother came closer. "It's on," she said.

Peter's parents came closer and closer. Their faces grew larger and larger until they filled the whole screen.

"He wouldn't leave without his game," said his mother.

"That's for sure," said his father.

As Peter watched, two giant hands reached toward the screen. They were Mr. Lenox's hands. The fingers closed around the side of the screen.

Suddenly, the screen bounced and jerked as Mr. Lenox lifted it.

Once again, Peter stared at his parents' faces.

"I can't imagine where he could have gone," said his mother.

"Well, we might as well turn this off," said his father.

No! Peter thought. *Don't!*

But it was too late. Everything went black.

Dead End

Everyone knew that Randall Glass was different. After he was born, his parents moved to the house across from Dead End Road. The big yellow sign at the beginning of the road said DEAD END. When Randall was just a baby and his mother pushed his stroller past that sign, he would always cry.

Later, if a ball rolled onto Dead End Road, he refused to get it. If his friends wanted to ride their bikes down the road, he refused to go.

But Randall was strange in other ways, too. He hated rooms with open windows. He refused to wear anything black. And instead of making a left turn, he would always make three rights. And he would never, ever go down Dead End Road.

When other kids asked why, Randall said, "Do you know what dead end means? It's where the dead end up."

"No, it doesn't," said the other kids. "It means a street that ends and doesn't go anywhere."

Randall shook his head as if they were wrong.

The other kids laughed and teased Randall. But it didn't matter.

David Walsh was Randall's only friend. David was as normal as Randall was strange. When people asked David why he was Randall's friend, he said that Randall was the best friend a kid could have.

When Randall was eight, he and his family moved away. When kids asked David where Randall and his family had gone, David said he didn't know.

"Let's go down here," Tyler Ross said one gray spring day when he and David were riding their bikes. They'd stopped at the entrance to Dead End

Road. Tyler was one of David's many friends. But none of them could replace Randall.

David shook his head.

"Why not?" asked Tyler.

The answer was that Randall had told him never to go down Dead End Road. But David didn't say that. He just shook his head.

"Scared?" Tyler said in a taunting way.

David didn't like kids who teased and taunted. That's why Tyler Ross would never be the kind of friend Randall had been.

"The only things I'm afraid of," David said, "are the things I *should* be afraid of."

"There's nothing scary about a dead end," said Tyler.

"Then go down there yourself," said David.

Tyler looked down Dead End Road. There were no houses on it. Just big old trees with long, bare, gnarled branches. The road was old and full of deep, muddy potholes.

"That road looks really bad," said Tyler. "I'll go down it another time."

The boys started to ride away. Coming toward

them was a dump truck towing a big yellow back-hoe. When the driver saw the boys, he slowed down and waved. David and Tyler stopped.

"You kids know where Dead End Road is?" the driver asked.

David pointed. "Down there. On the left."

"Why are you going there?" asked Tyler.

"We're gonna start digging foundations next week," the driver said.

"For houses?" Tyler guessed.

The driver nodded. "They're building a new housing development back there."

That Friday, David was eating lunch in the school cafeteria when a boy named Billy Leeds came up to him. Billy was a bully and a braggart. David didn't like him. With Billy was Tyler and a boy named Cameron.

"Tyler says you're scared to go down Dead End Road," Billy said.

David chewed his sandwich and didn't answer.

"We're going down there tonight," said Billy. "You want to come with us? Or are you afraid?"

"I'm only afraid of the things I *should* be afraid of," David answered.

"So you won't go?" Billy said.

David shook his head.

"You're chicken," said Billy.

"If you say so," said David.

It was warm that evening. As dark approached, David was outside, shooting baskets in his driveway. David loved basketball. His father had installed outdoor lights so that he could play in the dark. While he was outside, Billy, Tyler, and Cameron rode up.

"Still too scared to come with us?" Billy asked.

David didn't answer. He took another shot with the basketball.

"Chicken," Billy said. Then he and the others rode away, down Dead End Road.

David shot baskets for a little while longer. Then he sat down on the ball and waited in his driveway. He wondered why Randall had told him never to go down Dead End Road. He wondered why he'd never thought to ask.

After a while, he heard the scratchy sounds of tires and heavy breathing and grunts. A few moments later, Billy and Cameron raced past on their bikes so fast that they didn't notice David sitting on the basketball in his driveway. Their eyes were wide with fright.

A second later, David saw Tyler ride out of Dead End Road as fast as he could. Like the other boys, his eyes were wide with fear. David rose to his feet and waved, "Tyler!"

Tyler skidded to a stop on his bike. With wide eyes, he looked at David. Then he looked back at Dead End Road and bit his lip nervously. David walked toward him. Tyler was breathing hard and shaking.

"What happened?" David asked.

"We went down to the end," Tyler said. He was still panting. "The only thing down there was that big yellow backhoe and a field of tall weeds. I didn't like it. There was something creepy about that field. Billy got off his bike and said he wanted to walk into the field to see what was there. Cameron and I didn't want to, but Billy said we were chicken, so we did."

David nodded slowly. Not many boys could let themselves be called a chicken.

"So we walked out into the field," Tyler said. "It wasn't easy because the weeds were really thick and they came up past our knees. Our feet kept getting tangled and caught in them. It felt really creepy. Almost like hands reaching up and trying to grab our ankles. And the deeper into the field we went, the worse it was."

"Billy looked really scared just now when he rode past," David said.

"He was ahead of Cameron and me," Tyler said. "I don't know what happened, but the next thing I knew he let out a yell and started to run back to the bikes. Then Cameron and I were running, too. And every step felt like something was grabbing at our ankles. It was the scariest thing I ever felt. I was really happy to get out of there. And I don't blame you for not wanting to go."

Tyler looked back at the entrance to Dead End

Road. "I'll never go down there again. Right now I just want to go home and get into bed and stay there. See you, David."

David watched Tyler ride away. Then he went into his house.

The next day was Saturday. David was outside shooting baskets again when two police cars came down the street and turned onto Dead End Road. A little while later, more cars came. One car said COUNTY CORONER on its side.

Later, the truck turned off of Dead End Road towing the big yellow backhoe. David waved at the driver to stop.

"I thought you were going to dig foundations for that new development," David said.

"We started, but you won't believe what we found," the driver said. "That field is full of bones. It must be some kind of ancient burial ground. Strangest thing I ever saw. No sign saying it's a cemetery. No tombstones. A whole field of skeletons so close to the surface they could practically reach up and grab you. Not one of them was buried more than six inches deep. The police are down there, trying to figure out where they all came from."

The driver drove away, taking the big yellow backhoe with him. David glanced across the street at the sign that said DEAD END.

Randall was right, he thought. *It's where the dead end up.*

A Safe Place to Stay

Rain splashed against the car's windshield. Even with the windshield wipers swishing back and forth, it was almost impossible to see in the dark.

"We're lost," Mrs. Burke said to her husband.

"The sign on the highway said there was a gas station down this road," said Mr. Burke.

"We've gone at least ten miles," said Mrs. Burke. "I haven't seen a gas station."

"It has to be around here somewhere," said Mr. Burke.

"Why don't we just go back to the highway?" asked Ethan Burke. Ethan was twelve. His little sister, Sara, was eight. They were sitting in the backseat.

Mr. Burke stared at the gas gauge. The red warning light glowed. The needle had dipped below EMPTY. "I'm not sure we have enough gas to get back to the highway," he said. "And even if we did, we definitely don't have enough to make it to the next exit."

Crack! A bolt of lightning lit the sky.

"I'm scared!" Sara wailed in the backseat.

Boom! The crash of thunder from above made them all jump.

"Mommy!" Sara cried. Mrs. Burke reached over the seat and held her daughter's hand.

But there was good news. "I think I saw the gas station when the lightning struck," Mr. Burke said. "It's up ahead."

They drove a little farther in the pouring rain.

"There it is!" Ethan cried, pointing through the

windshield. While he didn't want to admit that he was afraid, he was very happy that he'd seen the station.

A moment later, the Burkes drove up to the gas station. But it was dark. The lights were off.

"It's closed," Mrs. Burke said.

"What'll we do?" asked Ethan.

"I don't know," his father answered, and looked at Mrs. Burke.

"We can't go back to the highway," said Mrs. Burke. "So I guess we'll have to find a place to stay for the night around here."

Mr. Burke peered out into the dark. All he could see was rain. "Where?" he asked.

"We'll have to look for a place," said his wife.

"I don't know if that's a good idea," Mr. Burke said. "What if we start driving and run out of gas before we find a place to stay? We'll be in the middle of nowhere. If we stay here, at least we'll be able to get gas when the station opens in the morning."

"You want to stay in the car all night?" Mrs. Burke asked.

"I don't want to do that!" Sara cried.

"I don't know what other choice we have," said Mr. Burke.

"I promised my sister we'd be at their house by ten in the morning," said Mrs. Burke.

"Let me check something," said Mr. Burke. He took a flashlight out of the glove compartment and then got out of the car. The rest of his family watched while he went up to the gas station door. He shined the flashlight around and then came back and got into the car.

"They open at six in the morning," Mr. Burke said. "If we fill up right at six, we should be able to get to your sister's house by ten."

"I don't want to stay in the car all night!" Sara wailed.

"I don't know what else we can do," said Mr. Burke.

The family sat in the car. The rain crashed down. All around them thunder boomed and lightning flashed and crackled.

"I'm scared!" Sara cried again.

"Come up here," Mrs. Burke said.

Sara climbed into the front seat and curled up in

her mother's lap. Mrs. Burke looked at her husband. "We can't stay like this all night."

Mr. Burke made a decision. He turned up the collar of his raincoat and reached for the flashlight again.

"Where are you going?" his wife asked.

"I'm going to walk down the road," said Mr. Burke.

"In the rain and dark?" Mrs. Burke said.

"I don't know how else to find a place where we can stay," her husband said, and started to open the door.

"Be careful!" Mrs. Burke said.

Mr. Burke got out of the car and turned on the flashlight. His family watched him disappear into the dark and rain.

"What if something happens to him?" Ethan asked nervously.

"Nothing bad is going to happen," Mrs. Burke assured him.

Mrs. Burke and her children waited in the car. The rain hammered down on the roof. Thunder crashed and lightning flashed outside. Ethan's stomach was in knots as he waited for his father to return.

"Why hasn't Daddy come back?" Sara asked after a while.

"I'm sure he's still looking," said Mrs. Burke.

The family waited and waited.

"Seems like he's been gone a long time," Ethan said nervously.

"I'm sure he's okay," replied Mrs. Burke. But inside she was worried, too.

More time passed. By now Sara had fallen asleep in Mrs. Burke's lap. Sara was a big girl for her age, and Mrs. Burke was very uncomfortable. She knew she couldn't spend the night like that.

"Mom, I'm scared," Ethan whispered, hoping he didn't wake up Sara. "Dad should have come back by now."

"Everything will be okay," Mrs. Burke said. But now she was scared, too.

They waited. The rain beat down. Ethan's eyelids grew heavy. But he didn't want to fall asleep.

"Ah!" Suddenly, Mrs. Burke gasped.

Ethan opened his eyes. A stranger was coming out of the dark!

Ethan tensed. He gripped the seat.

Outside, the stranger in the dark reached for the door.

"Mom, do something!" Ethan gasped.

The car door opened. Ethan's heart was pounding. The pouring rain roared.

The stranger stuck his head in through the open door.

It was Mr. Burke.

Ethan and his mother both sighed loudly with relief.

"You scared the daylights out of us," Mrs. Burke said.

"Sorry." Rainwater dripped off Mr. Burke's head and shoulders. "I've got good news." He held up a diamond-shaped piece of green plastic. A key was attached to it.

"You found a place to stay?" Mrs. Burke gasped with delight.

"Sure did," said Mr. Burke as he got into the car.

"It's just up the road." He handed Ethan the key. "Hold this."

"I thought hotels give you a key card," said Ethan.

"This is what they used to give you," said his father as he started to drive. "Back in the day."

Mr. Burke drove around the bend and up a muddy driveway. The car splashed through potholes as they went up a hill. Sara woke up. "What's happening?" she asked with a yawn.

"We're going to a place where we can sleep," said her mother.

The car bounced up the old driveway. The windshield wipers swished back and forth. Soon a row of small old brown cabins came into view.

"What is this?" Ethan asked.

"These are bungalows," explained his father. "This is the way motels were set up in the old days."

"The *real* old days," said Mrs. Burke.

Mr. Burke parked the car beside one of the bungalows. He opened the door and the family hurried through the rain and inside. The walls of the bungalow were made of yellow wood. The refrigerator was small and rounded. The kitchen table and chairs had metal legs.

"What's that funny smell?" Ethan asked.

"Propane," said Mr. Burke. "It's for the heater and the stove. No one uses it anymore."

"Why not?" Ethan asked.

"Too dangerous," said Mr. Burke. "Every now and then, a propane tank would explode."

"We're not in danger, are we?" asked Mrs. Burke.

"Not if we're staying here just one night," said Mr. Burke. "I mean, think of how old this place is. If it hasn't burned up yet, I'm sure it will last one more night."

"That's not funny," said Mrs. Burke.

"This place is way old," said Ethan.

"It's also way warm and dry and a lot more comfortable than spending the night in the car," said Mr. Burke. He checked his watch. "Enough talking. We better get to bed. We have to get up early and hit the road."

Sara slept on the couch. Ethan's parents took one bedroom and gave Ethan the other. Ethan slid into the bed. The sheets were rough and the blanket was scratchy. The pillow was hard and smelled like soap. But Ethan was tired and went right to sleep.

The next thing Ethan knew, his father was shaking his shoulder. Sunlight came in through the window. "Time to get up," Mr. Burke said. "We need to get going or we'll be late."

Still half asleep, Sara and Ethan climbed into the backseat of the car. It had stopped raining, and the sun had just risen over the distant hills. But the dirt driveway was still muddy.

"Don't you have to pay?" Mrs. Burke asked her husband.

"I paid last night," Mr. Burke said. "The owner told me to leave the key in the room when we left this morning."

Mr. Burke drove down the driveway and out onto the road. They went around the bend to the gas station. Even though the sun was out, rainwater still dripped off the gas station roof. Mr. Burke parked the car next to a gas pump. He checked his watch. "We're a few minutes early," he said.

The family waited in the car. Outside the sun continued to rise. At a few minutes after six A.M. an old red pickup truck pulled into the gas station. A large man with a gray beard and a red shirt got out. He frowned when he saw the Burkes' car.

Mr. Burke rolled down the car window. "Boy, are we glad to see you," he said.

"You haven't been here all night, have you?" the man asked.

"We got here last night, but you were closed," said Mr. Burke. "So we stayed in one of those bungalows around the bend."

The man's bushy gray eyebrows rose. "You did, did you?"

"Yes, sir," said Mr. Burke. "We all got a good night's sleep. And as soon as you fill up the tank, we'll be on our way."

The man started to fill the car's tank with gas. "Said you stayed in one of those bungalows, did you?" he said.

"Yes, sir," said Mr. Burke.

"The ones right around the corner?"

"That's correct," said Mr. Burke.

"Interesting," the man said, and finished pumping the gas.

Mr. Burke paid him. "Strange fellow," he said as they drove away from the gas station.

"Why do you say that, Dad?" Ethan asked.

"He acted like he didn't believe we stayed at those bungalows," said Mr. Burke.

"I wonder why," said Mrs. Burke.

They drove around the bend on their way back to the highway. As they passed the driveway to the bungalows, Ethan noticed something strange. "Dad, stop."

Mr. Burke stopped. A rusty, old metal gate crossed the driveway. It was held closed by a rusty chain. Up on the hill, all that remained of the bungalows were a few charred chimneys. Between them were the blackened stumps of trees.

Hanging on the locked gate was a sign that said CLOSED DUE TO FIRE.

Dance Lessons

"It's time for you to take dancing lessons," Mrs. Phelps said one night at dinner.

Stephen Phelps shook his head. "No way."

"It's what young men do when they enter the fifth grade," said his mother.

"Not me," said Stephen.

Mrs. Phelps glanced at her husband for help.

"I went when I was your age," his father said.

"And all your friends are going," added Mrs. Phelps.

The next day at school, Stephen asked his best friend, Gary Wells, if he was going to go.

"It's not a big deal," Gary said. "Everybody does it. You go for two hours on Friday nights, and then someone's mother or father takes us out for ice cream."

"What if you ask a girl to dance and she says no?" Stephen asked.

"It's not allowed," said Gary. "If you ask, they have to say yes."

Stephen wasn't convinced, but he decided to give it a try. That Friday night he put on a white shirt and a tie and his blue blazer.

"Have fun," Mr. Phelps said when he dropped Stephen off at the recreation center. Stephen doubted he'd have fun. When he saw the girls in their dresses and white gloves and black patent-leather shoes, he thought they looked silly. He felt a little better when he saw Gary arrive.

"What do we do?" Stephen asked nervously as they went inside.

"Just do whatever they tell you to do," Gary whispered.

An old lady named Miss Maples taught the lessons. A group of boys and girls from the high school acted as her assistants. The high school boys helped teach the fifth-grade girls, and the high school girls helped the fifth-grade boys.

Stephen did what he was told. They showed him how to ask a girl to dance and how to offer his hand.

But the best part of the dance lesson came later when Gary's mother took them all out for ice cream.

Each week, Stephen learned a little more about dancing, but he didn't like it. When it was time to practice, he wouldn't dance with a girl his own age. He would only dance with one of the older dance instructors. The best part of each lesson was always going out for ice cream with his friends.

No one told Stephen that the last lesson of the year was a real dance. That night, Stephen and Gary and the other boys stood on one side of the dance floor, and the girls stood on the other. The boys whispered and the girls giggled. The music started, and Miss Maples told the boys to cross the dance floor and ask a girl to dance. Stephen looked around. The high school boys and girls were sitting in chairs against the far wall. Tonight they weren't there to dance.

"You can't ask a high school girl to dance with you this time," Gary whispered in Stephen's ear. "You have to ask a girl our age."

Stephen felt a chill. So far he'd managed to avoid dancing with a girl his own age. All around him, boys bit their lips and stared at their feet. Across the floor, the girls stood in groups, whispering and giggling.

"Don't wait too long," Gary whispered. "The best dancers always get picked first."

One by one, the boys on Stephen's side of the room crossed the dance floor. Stephen froze. His forehead felt hot and his palms were moist. His feet wouldn't move.

"Time to go," Gary said, and started across the floor.

Stephen watched his friend walk up to a tall girl

with curly hair. Her name was Elise and she was a good dancer.

More and more boys were asking girls to dance. The floor began to fill with dancing couples. Gary was dancing with Elise, but he kept looking over at Stephen. Stephen knew his friend wanted him to pick a partner and dance. He knew that soon he would be the only one left.

But Stephen felt paralyzed. He knew that asking a girl to dance should not have been a big deal. It would be much worse to be the only boy left without a dance partner. If he danced, no one would care. But if he didn't dance, kids would talk about it at school tomorrow.

And yet, he couldn't get himself to ask.

Suddenly, a girl with long brown hair stepped through the doorway. She was wearing a yellow dress and white gloves and black shoes. Stephen had never seen her before. He didn't know who she was, but he knew she was the one he would dance with.

Stephen quickly crossed the floor. He was afraid some other boy might get there first. But no one did. He remembered how to introduce himself. The girl said her name was Dawn. Stephen asked her to dance and offered his hand. Her hand felt as light as a feather.

Stephen led her to the dance floor and held her the way he'd been taught. Soon they were moving together to the music. Dawn moved as lightly as an angel. As far as Stephen was concerned, she was the best dancer— and the prettiest girl— in the whole dance.

Together, Stephen and Dawn danced around the floor. Dawn followed his lead perfectly. Not once did she step on his foot, or did he step on hers. As they danced, other couples moved out of their way. Some kids smiled. Others frowned. Stephen knew that the ones who frowned were jealous because his partner was the best and prettiest dancer.

Stephen was sorry when the song ended. He didn't want the music to stop. He wanted to keep dancing with Dawn all night long. But it was now time for the boys to get their partners some refreshments. Stephen walked Dawn to the girls' side of the room and told her to wait while he got punch for both of them. Then he hurried to join the other boys around the punch bowl.

The other boys grinned and winked at him. Stephen smiled to himself. He knew they all wished they'd waited until Dawn arrived. Then Gary joined him by the punch bowl.

"What are you doing?" Gary hissed at his friend.

"I'm getting my partner some punch," Stephen said.

"What partner?" Gary whispered.

"Dawn," Stephen said. "The girl I was dancing with."

"You were dancing alone," Gary said.

"What are you talking about?" Stephen said. "Everyone saw me dancing with her."

"Everyone saw you dancing by yourself," Gary said. "Everyone thinks you're crazy."

"You're the one who's crazy," Stephen said. "Or should I say, jealous?"

Stephen picked up two cups of punch and headed back to the girls' side of the room. The girls smiled when he passed them. Some leaned toward their friends and whispered.

Stephen went back to the spot where he'd left Dawn, but she wasn't there. He looked around the room. He asked the girls if anyone had seen the pretty brown-haired girl in the yellow dress. No one had. He asked if they knew a girl named Dawn. No one did. He asked the high school kids and Miss Maples. No one had seen her. He went out into the hall, but it was empty. Then he went outside into the dark.

The sky was a checkerboard pattern of clouds and darkness. Stephen looked around, but all he saw were trees and parked cars.

"Dawn!" he yelled. "Dawn?"

There was no answer.

Stephen walked all the way around the center, calling Dawn's name.

No one answered.

By now, he knew she was gone.

He looked back at the building. The lights were on and he could hear music. The next song had begun. Everyone was dancing again. He knew if he went back, the kids would smile at him. Some would snicker. They would all think he was crazy.

Even worse, he would have to ask a different girl to dance.

Stephen knew he wasn't crazy. And the only girl he wanted to dance with was Dawn. She was real. He knew what she felt like and what she smelled like.

Stephen started to walk away from the center. "Dawn!" he called. "Dawn?"

He knew she was out there somewhere.

He just had to find her.

Nighttime ™
Too Scared to Sleep

Nighttime™
Too Scared to Sleep

by Todd Strasser

Scholastic Inc.

New York   Toronto   London   Auckland   Sydney
Mexico City   New Delhi   Hong Kong   Buenos Aires

To Elena's daughter, Melanie
—T.S.

ISBN-13: 978-0-439-80067-9
ISBN-10: 0-439-80067-6

Text copyright © 2007 by Todd Strasser
Illustrations copyright © 2007 by Scholastic Inc.

12 11 10 9 8 7 6 5 4 3 2 1   7 8 9 10 11 12/0

Printed in the U.S.A.
First printing, October 2007

CONTENTS

Whispers in the Dark

"You have to share your room with Megan," Mrs. Pickler said. She was holding the new baby in her arms. The baby's name was Peter. Megan was Billy Pickler's little sister.

"No!" Billy said. He crossed his arms and buried his chin against his chest.

"You'll only have to share for a few months," said his mother. "Just until we move to our new house."

"No!" Billy yelled.

"Billy, that's very selfish of you," scolded Mr. Pickler. "Megan's room is going to be the nursery for Peter. She has to move out. You get to keep your room. She can stay with you for a few months. I expect you to act like a big boy and help us with this."

Billy didn't want to help. The new baby was a big pain. All Peter did was cry. Everybody made a big fuss about him. And Megan was annoying. Billy didn't want her moving into his room. Mrs. Pickler whispered something to her husband.

"Come on, Billy," Mr. Pickler said. "Let's go play catch."

Billy and his father went to the park. Then Mr. Pickler bought him an ice cream. But when Mr. Pickler brought Billy home, there was an extra bed in Billy's bedroom. Megan was putting her dolls on the shelf above it.

"No!" Billy yelled. "I don't want those dolls in my room!"

"I need my dolls!" Megan cried.

"Not in my room!" Billy shouted.

Both kids started to scream. Finally, Mr. and

Mrs. Pickler made a decision. Megan would have one half of the room. Billy would have the other half. Megan would be allowed to keep two dolls on her shelf. She chose Jade and Cloe.

Billy refused to go into his room for the rest of the day. He hated dolls more than anything in the world.

That night, Megan went to bed at eight P.M. She was sound asleep when Billy's parents told him he had to go to bed. Billy went to his room. He was still angry that he had to share his room with his sister. And he was *very* angry that she had put her dolls on the shelf. He was so angry that he couldn't fall asleep.

Billy decided to sit in bed and read. He opened his favorite book, *The Scariest Stories Ever*. But when Billy started to read, he felt something strange. It felt as if he and his sister weren't the only ones in the room. Billy imagined that the dolls on the shelf were staring at him. They looked like they wanted to laugh because they got to be in his room and there was nothing Billy could do about it.

That just made Billy angrier. He decided to put

his two favorite wrestling action figures on the shelf across from the dolls. He made sure they were staring back. Then he fell asleep.

The next afternoon, Megan had a playdate at a friend's house. Billy sat on the floor in his room playing with his wrestlers. But he could feel the eyes of his sister's dolls on him. He hated those dolls. And so did his wrestlers.

Billy had an idea. His parents had said he wasn't allowed to go into his sister's half of the room. But they'd said nothing about his action figures. With one wrestler in each hand, Billy reached across and took the blonde Cloe doll from the shelf.

Billy let his wrestlers twist the doll's head around. They stomped on Cloe's legs and body-slammed her to the ground. Billy felt happy. Those dolls were getting what they deserved. Then Billy heard the door open and close downstairs. He quickly put Cloe back on her shelf. Soon Megan came into the room. But she had no idea what had happened.

That night, Billy felt happy when he went to bed. His wrestlers had taught those dolls a lesson.

They wouldn't laugh at him again. He turned off the light and closed his eyes and started to fall asleep.

"Psssst!" Billy thought he heard something. It sounded like an angry whisper. Very softly, a girl's voice said, "You shouldn't have done that."

Billy opened his eyes. He sat up in bed and turned on the light. He quickly looked around, but he didn't see anyone else in the room. Megan was in her bed, sleeping soundly. Her dolls sat on the shelf. *Wait a minute!* Was it Billy's imagination, or did they look like they were frowning?

No, it couldn't be. Billy turned off the light and went to sleep.

The next afternoon, Mrs. Pickler took Megan to her skating lesson. Once again Billy played with his wrestlers in his room. This time, he had them take the dark-haired Jade doll from the shelf. Billy made the wrestlers twist her arms and legs. They put her in a sleeper hold. Just before Megan got home, he put the Jade doll back on the shelf.

That night, Megan went to bed at eight o'clock

again. When Billy went to bed, he turned off the light and snuggled under his blanket. He was almost asleep when he heard a girl whisper, "I've had enough of this."

And another voice angrily agreed. "It's time to put a stop to it."

Billy sat up and turned on the lights. This time, he was certain he'd heard a voice. His heart began to beat hard. He had to stop himself from running into his parents' bedroom. Nothing in the room looked different. Megan was in her bed, sleeping soundly. Billy wondered if he had imagined the whispers. Maybe it was a dream. The dolls sat on the shelf facing him. Did they look angry? Billy rolled over and turned his back to them. He tried to go back to sleep.

That night, Billy had a strange dream. There were tiny footsteps and the sounds of girls whispering. He dreamed he heard light scratching and soft grunts. Two small figures moved in the shadows.

In the morning, Billy and Megan got dressed. Megan went downstairs for breakfast. Billy started to follow. Then he remembered a book he needed for school. He went back to the bedroom. As he reached for the book, he glanced at his wrestlers.

Their hands were tied behind their backs.

Billy looked at Cloe and Jade on his sister's shelf.

He was certain they were smiling.

Halloween Music

"Andy!" yelled Michael.

"Hey, Andy!" called Zach.

"Earth to Andy!" said Garrett.

Andy Stone walked away down the sidewalk. He and his friends were carrying pillowcases. It was Halloween and they were trick-or-treating. But Andy's pillowcase was only half as full as the others'. His friends stood in a driveway and watched him walk away.

"Why does he keep wandering off?" Zach asked.

"Because he's listening to his iPod," Garrett said. "He always turns it up too loud. He must be the only kid in the world who likes music more than candy."

Andy kept walking. A thin white wire rose from his iPod to the small white earbuds in his ears.

"It's your turn to get him," Michael said to Zach.

"No way," said Zach. "I got him last time. It's Garrett's turn."

"OK," said Garrett, "but this is the last time. Next time he wanders off, I say we let him go."

Garrett went to get Andy, and the four boys continued trick-or-treating. But a few houses later, Andy wandered off again.

"That's it," Garrett muttered. "I'm tired of running after him. He's got to learn to pay attention."

"I've got an idea," whispered Zach.

A little while later, all four boys walked down a dark, shadowy street. A lone streetlight flickered. Only one house stood on this block. It was big and empty. The Marbury family had once lived there. But that was many years ago. The rusty gate creaked loudly when Michael pushed it open. The four boys went up the walk. They crossed the rotten old porch and pushed open the squeaky old door. Inside, the house was dark and smelled musty. Cobwebs hung in the doorways.

Andy stopped in the front hall and turned down the volume on his iPod. "What are we doing in here?" he asked.

"There's supposed to be a big barrel of candy hidden somewhere in this house," said Zach.

"But no one lives here," Andy said.

"Right," said Michael. "That's why they hid the barrel here."

That sounded strange to Andy. But he didn't really care. It was OK if his friends wanted to look for some mysterious barrel. He turned up the volume on his iPod and went with them.

"Let's make sure we stick together," said Zach.

The boys pretended to search the first floor. Then they headed upstairs. Sure enough, Andy wandered off down a hall, listening to his music.

"OK, guys," Zach whispered to Michael and Garrett. "Let's go outside and see what happens."

Andy listened to his iPod and strolled down a dark hallway inside the house. The air was chilly. Many of the windows were cracked or broken. Everything was old and dusty. Drafts made the cobwebs move. Most of the rooms were empty. Here and there, a table or chair was covered by an old white sheet.

To Andy, the whole place was just plain creepy. He got to the end of the hall and looked around. He doubted there was a barrel of candy in the house. And where were Zach, Garrett, and Michael, anyway?

"Guys?" Andy pulled the earbuds from his ears. "Hey, guys?"

No one answered. Suddenly, Andy knew he was alone. He felt a chill and his pulse began to race. The house was big and dark and scary. He wasn't sure he could find his way out. He walked back down the hall and called nervously. "Guys? *Guys!?*"

"Who's yelling?" a woman's voice asked.

Andy stopped and looked in the room the voice had come from. A beautiful young woman sat in a chair, lit by moonlight coming through a window. Her long red hair fell down over the shoulders of her long white dress. The moonlight made her glow.

"Who are you?" she asked.

"I'm Andy Stone. Who are you?"

"I'm Marjory Marbury," the woman said. "Did you come to visit?"

"Well, uh, I'm looking for my friends. They came here looking for candy."

Marjory Marbury blinked and sat up. "My goodness, you're right! It's Halloween."

"You didn't know that?" Andy asked.

"Forgive me," said the beautiful woman. "I always forget. Please help yourself." She pointed at a bowl on the table beside her. "And thank you for coming. I haven't had a visitor in so long."

Andy stepped closer and looked in the bowl. He frowned. He'd never seen candy like this before. "What is that?"

"Sweets, of course," said Marjory Marbury. "This

is rock candy, and this is licorice, and these are taffy. Please try some."

Marjory Marbury may have looked young, but she spoke the way people did in old black-and-white movies. Andy tried what she handed to him. The rock candy tasted sweet, like sugar. The licorice was strong, almost like cough syrup. When he put the taffy in his mouth, it felt hard. But soon it became chewy. "Can I take some to show my friends?" Andy asked. "I bet they've never seen candy like this."

"Certainly, you may," said Marjory. She looked at Andy and frowned. "What is that thing around your neck?"

"It's an iPod," Andy said.

"What does it do?" asked the woman.

Andy thought it was strange that she didn't know what an iPod was. But it was also strange that she was sitting in a dark room wearing a long white dress. And it was strange that she had offered him this odd candy. Andy took the earbuds from around his neck. "Put one in each ear."

Marjory Marbury did as he said. Andy picked

a song and played it for her. The woman's eyes widened with surprise. Then she gasped, "How marvelous!"

Andy's friends waited on the dark sidewalk outside the house.

"He's been in there a long time," said Garrett. "He must have noticed we're not there."

"He should have come out by now," Zach said nervously.

"It's pretty dark in there," said Michael. "What if he fell down the stairs?"

"We better go back in and find him," said Garrett.

The boys went through the creaky gate and up the walk. They crossed the old porch and went into the house.

Inside, Zach yelled, "Andy?"

Upstairs, Andy heard his friend call. Marjory Marbury was still listening to the music. Andy wanted his friends to meet her, so he went to the doorway and called, "Up here."

Garrett, Michael, and Zach climbed the stairs. They found Andy waiting for them in the hall.

"Why are you still in here?" Michael asked.

"We were worried something happened to you," said Garrett.

"I was just showing this lady my iPod," Andy said. "Can you believe she's never heard of an iPod?"

Andy's friends looked puzzled. "What are you talking about?"

"Marjory Marbury." Andy turned to show them the woman in the white dress.

But the woman was gone. Andy's iPod lay on the empty chair. Andy looked around the moonlit room. There was no sign of Marjory Marbury anywhere. He walked over to the chair and picked up the iPod. "She was sitting right here," he said. He looked in the bowl, but it was empty. "She gave me some strange candy from this bowl."

"Very funny, Andy," said Zach. "Marjory Marbury's dead."

"No, she isn't," Andy said. "She was right here."

"No way," said Zach. "She died sixty years ago. And guess how?"

"How?" asked Michael.

"She choked to death on a piece of candy," said Zach. "On Halloween night."

"That's impossible," Andy said. "I was just talking to her. She must have left when you guys came in."

Zach shook his head slowly. "There's only one flight of stairs. We would have seen her."

Andy felt a chill. His friend was right.

"Let's get out of here," said Garrett. "I want to keep on trick-or-treating."

Andy glanced one more time around the room. He didn't understand where Marjory Marbury could have gone. "I'm telling you. She was right there in that chair."

"Sure, Andy," said Zach.

"Whatever you say, Andy," said Garrett.

Andy followed his friends down the stairs and out of the old house.

"Just do us a favor and don't wander off again, OK?" said Michael.

Andy followed his friends down the sidewalk. He knew they'd never believe that Marjory Marbury had been there. For the rest of the night, he stayed close to his friends.

It wasn't until he got home that he put his hand in his jacket pocket. Inside were the rock candy, taffy, and pieces of licorice.

Only a Dream

Samantha Stevens tossed and turned in bed. She was having a bad dream. In the dream, she went into her parents' room. But her parents weren't there. A strange couple was. The woman sitting at the makeup table had blonde hair. Samantha's mother had dark hair. A man sat on the corner of the bed tying his shoes. But the man wasn't Samantha's father.

Samantha woke in the middle of the night and ran crying into her parents' room.

"What's wrong?" Mr. Stevens asked after turning on his reading light.

"I had a bad dream," Samantha cried. She put her arms around her father's neck and hugged him. "I dreamed I went into your room and there were two strange people there."

"It's just your mom and me," her father said.

Samantha's mother turned on her lamp. "Don't be scared," she said.

Samantha saw that it was her parents. She felt better.

"Go back to bed," said Mr. Stevens. "Everything will be OK."

Samantha went back to her room. The light was off. She didn't like to go into her room when it was dark, but she wanted to be brave. She got into bed. Soon she was asleep.

But once again, she had a bad dream. This time, the strange couple was sleeping in her parents' bed. Samantha woke up. Her heart was drumming, and she was breathing fast. The dream felt very real. Samantha didn't care about being brave. For the second time that night, she ran into her parents' bedroom crying. She had to be sure that her parents were really there.

Once again, her parents turned on their lights.

"Did you have another bad dream?" asked her mother.

Samantha nodded. "I dreamed there were two strangers sleeping in your bed," she said.

"That sounds very frightening," said Mr. Stevens. "But now you've come in twice, and who have you found?"

"You and Mom," Samantha answered.

"So if you have that dream again, what will you know?" asked her father.

"That it was only a dream," said Samantha.

"Yes," said Mr. Stevens. "No matter how many times you have that dream, the only people you will find are your mom and me."

This time, Mrs. Stevens brought Samantha back to her room. "I know it's a very scary dream," she said as she tucked her daughter into bed. "But I want you to be a big, brave girl. If you have that dream again and wake up, what should you do?"

"Stay in bed," answered Samantha.

"That's right," said Mrs. Stevens. "Remember, it's only a dream."

She kissed Samantha on the forehead and then left the room.

A few minutes later, Samantha fell asleep. This time, she dreamed it was morning. The strange couple was in her parents' bedroom, making the bed. Samantha woke up. Her heart was beating very hard. Once again, the dream had felt so real. She wanted to jump out of bed to run to her parents' room. Then she remembered what her mother had said about being a big, brave girl. So even though she felt very frightened, Samantha stayed in bed.

It wasn't long before she fell asleep.

This time, she didn't dream about the strangers.

In the morning, Samantha opened her eyes. Her bedroom was filled with sunlight. Samantha was glad the night was over. She jumped out of bed and rushed to her parents' bedroom. She wanted to tell them that she'd stayed in bed even though she had the bad dream again.

Her parents' bed was made, but her parents weren't there. Samantha knew they had already gotten dressed and gone downstairs. She ran down the stairs and into the kitchen.

A man was sitting at the table, reading the newspaper.

A woman was sipping coffee.

They weren't her parents.

They were the strangers Samantha had dreamed about.

Witch Way

"We're going on a campout," said Mr. Sloan. It was Saturday morning. He was standing in the doorway of the TV room. His son, Paul, sat on the couch playing his PSP. Paul's younger sister, Amy, sat on the other end of the couch. She was watching a show on Nickelodeon. They were both in their pajamas.

"Did you hear me?" asked Mr. Sloan.

Neither child answered. Their eyes were glued

to the screens. Mr. Sloan stepped in front of the TV and turned it off. "When I speak to you I expect an answer."

"Hey!" Amy yelled. "It was the middle of a show."

"Why'd you do that?" complained Paul.

"I was talking, but you weren't listening," Mr. Sloan said sternly. "We're going on a campout."

"But it's cold," Amy said.

"It's going to get warmer this afternoon," said Mr. Sloan.

"What if it rains?" asked Paul.

"There's no rain in the forecast," replied his father.

"You always say that the weatherman is wrong," said Paul.

"He's not wrong today. We're leaving in half an hour," said Mr. Sloan. "Get dressed and help me load the car."

Half an hour passed, but Paul and Amy didn't get dressed. Amy spent the time looking at a catalog of dolls' clothes. Paul played with army men in his room. Mr. Sloan got mad. He told Paul that if he didn't get dressed right away he'd lose his allowance for two weeks. And Amy would not be allowed to go to her best friend's birthday party next weekend.

Both kids complained loudly, but they did get dressed. A little while later, they were sitting in the backseat of the car. Their parents sat in the front. Mr. Sloan backed the car out of the driveway. "Here we go!"

"Can we watch videos?" Paul asked.

"Today we're going to be electronics-free," said his mother.

"Boring," Amy grumbled.

Sometime later, Mr. Sloan parked the car in a gravel lot. It was a warm fall day. Gold and red leaves fluttered down from the trees, and the sky was blue.

Mr. Sloan took a deep breath and exhaled. "Doesn't that air smell good?"

Paul and Amy didn't answer. It smelled like plain old air to them.

"Grab your backpacks," said Mr. Sloan. "We'll hike along Witch Way to the campground."

The family began to hike through the woods.

"How much longer?" Amy soon asked.

"A while," said Mr. Sloan.

"My knees hurt," Paul complained.

"Let's see how they feel in a few minutes," said Mrs. Sloan.

"This is boring," said Amy.

Finally, the family stopped for a rest. "Anyone thirsty?" Mr. Sloan asked.

"I'll take a Coke," said Amy.

"All we have is water," said Mr. Sloan.

"I'm hungry," said Paul.

"We have trail mix and fresh carrots and apples," said Mrs. Sloan.

"Can I have a cookie?" asked Amy.

"We didn't bring any sweets," said Mr. Sloan.

"This stinks," Paul grumbled. But he took some trail mix.

While his family rested, Mr. Sloan looked around. He noticed an old cottage in the woods. The windows were broken and the front door was open. A crumbling chimney poked through the sagging roof. Mr. Sloan had hiked Witch Way many times before. He wondered why he'd never noticed the cottage.

The Sloan family started walking again. The hike should have taken an hour and a half. But the children walked slowly and complained often. They made many stops. It was getting dark by the time they reached the campsite. The air felt chilly. The Sloan children sat down on an old log.

"I'm hungry," Paul complained.

"I'm cold," said Amy.

"We'll start a fire and have dinner soon," said Mr. Sloan. "But first, we have to pitch the tent."

"Can't we eat first?" asked Paul.

"It's hard to pitch the tent in the dark," said Mr. Sloan. "If you help with the tent, we can eat sooner."

"I'm too hungry to help," said Paul.

"And I'm too cold," said Amy.

Mr. and Mrs. Sloan pitched the tent by themselves. Then Mr. Sloan went to find wood while Mrs. Sloan prepared dinner. The family sat around the campfire. Mrs. Sloan gave the children metal trail bowls filled with steaming beef stew.

Paul tasted the food and made a face. "This tastes awful!"

Both children refused to take another bite. By now Mr. Sloan was sorry that he'd brought his children on the campout. He decided to tell them a story that might teach them a lesson. "Have you ever heard the story of Hansel and Gretel?" he asked.

The children shook their heads.

"Once upon a time a poor woodcutter lived in the woods with his wife and two children," Mr. Sloan said. "The children's names were Hansel and Gretel."

"Those are weird names," said Amy.

"The woodcutter was very poor," said Mr. Sloan. "He couldn't find enough food for his family. They were slowly starving."

"Like me," grumbled Paul.

"One night, the woodcutter and his wife lay awake in their bed," said Mr. Sloan. "They were too hungry to sleep. His wife said, 'Tomorrow you must take the children deep into the woods and leave them.'

"'But then they will perish,' said the woodcutter.

"'If we don't get rid of them we will all starve,' his wife warned."

"Parents would never do that," said Paul.

"Would they?" asked Amy uncertainly.

"The woodcutter and his wife didn't know that their children were also too hungry to sleep that night," said Mr. Sloan. "They heard what their parents were planning. The next morning, Hansel put a piece of stale bread into his pocket. When the woodcutter led his children into the woods, Hansel left a trail of crumbs."

"So they could find their way back!" Paul realized.

Mr. Sloan nodded. "When they were very deep in the woods, the woodcutter turned to Hansel and Gretel. He had tears in his eyes. He told them to wait while he went to look for a tree to chop down. Then he left."

"What were they wearing?" Amy asked.

"Hansel was wearing lederhosen," said Mrs. Sloan.

"What's that?" asked Paul.

"Leather shorts," said Mrs. Sloan. "And they usually come with leather suspenders."

"What about Gretel?" asked Amy.

"She was wearing a dress and a white head scarf," said Mrs. Sloan.

Mr. Sloan continued the story. "The children waited for their father to return, but he never came back. Finally, Hansel told Gretel it was time to follow the trail of crumbs back home. They started to walk, but the crumbs had disappeared. Hansel heard the birds chirping in the trees. He realized they had eaten the crumbs."

"So the children couldn't find their way home," Amy realized.

"That's right," said Mr. Sloan.

"What did they do?" asked Paul.

"They had to spend the whole night in the dark woods," said Mr. Sloan.

"Where did they sleep?" asked Amy.

"They pushed together some leaves and lay down on them," said Mr. Sloan.

"I couldn't sleep like that," said Paul.

"It was cold and Hansel and Gretel shivered all night," said Mr. Sloan. "They barely slept. The next morning, Hansel and Gretel were hungry and miserable. Suddenly, the scent of gingerbread floated through the air. Gretel and her brother both smelled it."

"I know!" Amy gasped. "The woodcutter's wife made the gingerbread so that her children could follow the smell back home."

Mr. Sloan shook his head slowly. "Hansel and Gretel followed the smell. But it didn't lead them home. It led them to a small cottage in the deepest part of the woods. Only this was no ordinary cottage. It was made of gingerbread, and decorated with gumdrops and candy canes and other candies."

"Sour Power?" Paul asked eagerly, since that was his favorite.

"Maybe," said Mr. Sloan. "The candy was very tempting to the starving boy and girl. Hansel and Gretel were scared because they didn't know whose house it was. But their hunger was so great that they couldn't stop themselves from crawling close and nibbling."

"Something bad is going to happen," said Paul.

Mr. Sloan nodded. "A witch lived in the house. And she caught Hansel and Gretel and ate them."

"Really?" Amy jumped up and ran into her mother's arms. "That's not going to happen to us, is it?" she cried.

"No." Mrs. Sloan hugged her daughter. "And that's not how the story really goes. A witch did live in the house. And she wanted to eat the children. But they were too thin. So she fattened them up with good food. But just when she was ready to eat them, Gretel pushed her into the hot stove. Hansel and Gretel found lots of valuable jewels in the witch's house. They took the jewels home, and after that the woodcutter always had enough money for food."

Paul yawned. "Good story."

The fire had burned down. Red ashes glowed in the dark.

"Time for bed," said Mr. Sloan.

The Sloan family went into their tent. Each of them crawled into a sleeping bag and fell asleep.

Heh! Heh! Heeeehh!

In the middle of the night, an eerie laugh woke all of them.

Heh! Heh! Heeeehh!

"What's that?" Amy gasped.

"Must be an animal," said Mr. Sloan. "Don't worry, it won't bother us. Let's go back to sleep."

But before they could set their heads down, the laugh returned. *Heh! Heh! Heeeehh!*

"That's no animal, Dad," Paul said nervously. "It sounds like a witch's laugh."

"I'm scared!" cried Amy.

Mrs. Sloan reached for her daughter. "Come close," she said. "No one's going to hurt you."

Heh! Heh! Heeeehh!

"Mom!" Amy cried again. Mrs. Sloan hugged her daughter.

Paul was scared. "What's going on, Dad?"

Mr. Sloan's heart was beating hard. He had never

heard that sound in the woods before. "Everything's going to be OK. It has to be some kind of animal."

"Or a witch who wants to eat us," Amy wailed.

Mrs. Sloan held her daughter close. "No one's going to eat you." She looked at her husband in the dark. "Are they?"

"No, of course not," said Mr. Sloan.

With eyes wide open, they all lay in their sleeping bags. Hours passed before anyone in the Sloan family could fall asleep.

In the morning, Paul and Amy wanted to go home right away.

"Why don't we make some breakfast first?" asked Mr. Sloan.

"I don't want breakfast," said Amy. "I just want to go home. I'm never going hiking again."

"I think we should go," Mrs. Sloan agreed.

Amy helped her mother pack up the sleeping bags. Paul helped his father fold the tent.

"See how the work goes faster when everyone helps?" said Mr. Sloan when they were finished.

"Too bad they'll never go on a campout again," said Mrs. Sloan.

"Oh, come on," said Mr. Sloan. "It was just a story."

"What about that weird laughter?" asked Paul.

"Just some animal," Mr. Sloan insisted.

The Sloan family pulled on their backpacks and started down the trail. Paul and Amy walked quickly. They didn't complain or ask to rest.

Suddenly, Mrs. Sloan stopped. "Do you smell that?"

Mr. Sloan and the children took deep sniffs.

"I smell it!" said Amy.

"Me, too," said Paul. "It smells like . . ."

"Gingerbread," said Mrs. Sloan.

The family looked nervously at one another.

"That's weird," said Paul.

"I'm scared," said Amy.

"There's nothing to be afraid of," said Mr. Sloan. "I'm sure it's just a coincidence."

The family continued down the trail. The scent of gingerbread grew stronger and stronger. Mrs. Sloan and the children looked nervously at Mr. Sloan.

"It has to be a coincidence," Mr. Sloan insisted again. But then he stopped. Through the trees, he saw the old cottage with the broken windows. Smoke curled out of the chimney.

"Oh, my gosh!" Amy gasped, and pointed at the front steps of the house.

Lying on the ground were a pair of lederhosen and a white head scarf.

It's Just Wallpaper

"Do you like your new wallpaper?" Mrs. Andersen asked at bedtime on a windy fall night.

Sitting in bed, Courtney Andersen nodded. The old wallpaper had been bright orange, red, and yellow circus scenes. The clowns and lions and dancing bears had scared her. The new wallpaper had green, brown, and blue scenes of children playing in a park. Instead of cages and lion tamers, there were trees and swings.

"I'm glad," said Mrs. Andersen. "You can read for a little while, but lights off at eight thirty."

Courtney picked up her book and began to read. But as soon as her mother left the bedroom, she put the book down and looked at the wallpaper. The boys and girls were riding bicycles, swinging on tree swings, and jumping rope. A boy with brown hair was skateboarding in a playground. Nearby, a pretty blonde girl with a blue ribbon in her hair was riding a bike.

Courtney looked down at her book and began to read again. But then she stopped. Something about the wallpaper bothered her. She looked at it again. Was the boy on the skateboard staring at the pretty girl on the bike? Courtney got on her knees and looked more closely. Was he frowning? Did he look angry?

Courtney got back under the covers and read. Soon Mrs. Andersen knocked on the door and told her to go to sleep. Courtney turned off the light and lay in the dark. In her mind, the brown-haired boy was skating across the playground toward the pretty girl on the bike. The pretty girl didn't see him coming. The brown-haired boy was getting closer and closer.

Suddenly, Courtney felt scared. She jumped out of bed and ran into her parents' room.

Her mother was sitting in bed, reading a book. Mr. Andersen was sitting next to her. He was watching a basketball game on television. Mrs. Andersen lifted her reading glasses and asked, "What's wrong, honey?"

"The boy in the wallpaper," Courtney said. "He's going to hurt the girl on the bike."

Mrs. Andersen turned and gave her husband a look.

Mr. Andersen got out of bed. "Let's see."

In her bedroom, Courtney showed her father the boy on the wallpaper.

"I see what you mean," Mr. Andersen said. "It does seem as if he's looking at the girl on the bike. But has he really gotten closer to her?"

Courtney studied the wallpaper. It did not look like the boy on the skateboard was closer to the girl.

Mr. Andersen smiled. "OK, now turn off the light and go to sleep. It's just wallpaper."

Courtney did as she was told. But as soon as she closed her eyes, she could see the boy skating closer and closer to the girl on the bike. She could even hear the scrape of the skateboard's wheels on the pavement!

Frightened, Courtney jumped out of bed and ran into her parents' room. "I can hear him!" she gasped.

Once again, Mr. Andersen returned with his daughter to her room. They looked at the wallpaper together. "Does he really look closer to her?"

Courtney shook her head.

"It's just your imagination," said Mr. Andersen.

"But I heard him," she said.

Mr. Andersen sat on the corner of her bed and listened. Now he knew what his daughter had heard. "It's the branches scraping against the side of the house in the wind."

Courtney listened. Her father was right. It was just the wind. She felt a little silly. "I'm sorry, Daddy."

"It's OK." Mr. Andersen tucked his daughter into

bed. He kissed her on the forehead. "Now go to sleep. Everything is going to be all right."

"Would you leave the door open a little and the light on in the hall?" Courtney asked.

"Of course." Mr. Andersen left the door open and went back to his bedroom.

Courtney lay in bed and listened to the branches scrape against the house. Soon her eyes closed and she fell asleep.

The light coming through the doorway lit the wallpaper.

Children laughed as they swung on the swings.

Skateboard wheels scraped the pavement.

A pretty blonde girl hummed to herself as she rode her bicycle.

From the shadows came a crash and a girl's cry.

The pretty blonde girl sat on the pavement with tears in her eyes.

Nearby, a skateboard lay upside down.

The boy with the brown hair rode away on her bike.

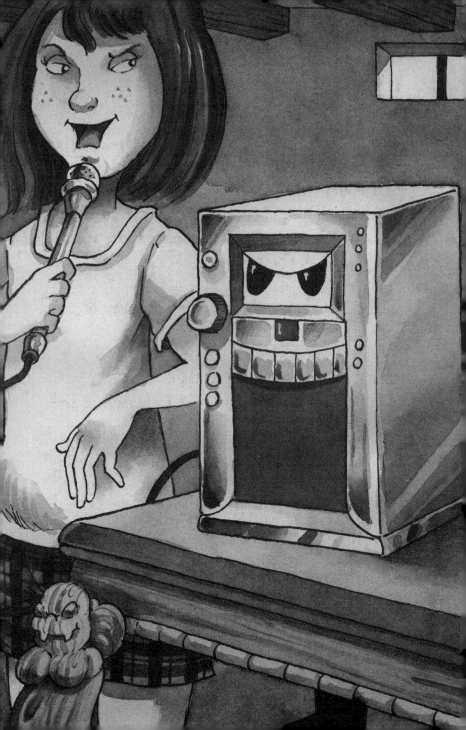

Don't Sleep Over

Kara Green was mad. "Why do I have to invite Dana Merrill to my sleepover?" she asked her mother.

"Because it's the right thing to do," answered Mrs. Green. "If you want to borrow the Merrills' karaoke machine for your sleepover, then you should invite Dana, too."

Kara balled her hands into fists and frowned. Her

red hair hung down to her shoulders. Her freckles turned pale when she was angry. "Dana Merrill is a loser."

Mrs. Green looked up from her computer. "That's not nice, Kara."

"But it's true!" Kara insisted. "Wait until the other girls find out she's invited. None of them will want to come to my party. My sleepover will be ruined!" Kara blinked hard and made tears come to her eyes.

Mrs. Green lowered her glasses. "Your friends will come to the party because they're your friends," she said calmly.

"Mom, *please* don't make me invite Dana," Kara begged.

Mrs. Green sighed and gazed up at the ceiling. Kara knew that her mother was thinking. She crossed her fingers.

But Mrs. Green looked back at Kara and shook her head. "I'm sorry, Kara. If you want the karaoke machine, you have to invite Dana."

Kara narrowed her eyes and spun around. She stormed out of the room, making sure the door banged loudly behind her. She was already coming up with a plan.

She would invite Dana Merrill to her sleepover. But that didn't mean Dana had to stay.

The night of the sleepover arrived. Kara and her friends carried their sleeping bags downstairs. The basement had soft gray carpeting and a long, comfortable black couch. Mr. Green's exercise bicycle stood in one corner. In another corner were tennis rackets, baseball bats and mitts, skis and boots.

Dana Merrill was the last girl to come down the steps and into the basement. Kara had already shared her plan with her friends. Everyone agreed to ignore Dana. When they sang along with the karaoke machine, Dana didn't get a chance to sing. When they laid out their sleeping bags on the floor, there was no room for Dana's. She had to lay hers down on the other side of the couch.

The girls ignored Dana until she burst into tears and ran upstairs. She begged Mrs. Green to take her home.

Back in the basement, Kara smiled and said, "Good riddance."

Mrs. Green came downstairs to the basement at ten o'clock. She told the girls to turn off the karaoke machine and get into their sleeping bags. Kara could see that her mother was upset that Dana had gone home in tears. But Kara didn't care. It was her mother's fault for insisting that Dana be invited.

The girls crawled into their sleeping bags. Mrs. Green climbed to the top of the stairs and turned off the basement lights. Because it was nighttime outside, the basement was very dark. The girls couldn't see their hands in front of their eyes.

"It's too dark," a girl named Jill whispered nervously.

"Anyone know any scary stories?" whispered a girl named Robyn. She was bigger and stronger than the other girls. Some of them were afraid of her.

"Oh, please don't!" Jill begged. "I'm already scared."

Kara was glad that Jill admitted she was afraid. This was the first time that Kara had spent the night in a basement. She was a little scared, too. But she didn't want to admit it.

Kara's friend Randi had packed a small flashlight. She turned it on. The beam wasn't very strong. But the girls could see one another in the faint light.

"Afraid of the dark, Randi?" Robyn asked in a taunting voice.

"No, I just like to see everyone," Randi answered.

The girls lay in the dim light for a while. They talked about school and clothes and their favorite TV stars. One by one they stopped talking and drifted off into sleep.

Soon the basement was dark and still. The girls slept peacefully in their sleeping bags. Then, suddenly, the karaoke machine went on.

Who's the meanest girl of all?
Is she short or is she tall?

Kara opened her eyes. Randi turned on her little flashlight. The other girls opened their eyes, too.

The red and white lights on the karaoke machine glowed in the dark.

"Who turned it on?" asked Robyn.

"Not me," said Jill.

"Not me," said Randi.

"What about you, Kara?" Robyn asked.

"Not me," said Kara.

"One of you is lying," said Robyn.

Kara got out of her sleeping bag and turned the machine off. Soon the girls were once again asleep.

Who's the meanest girl of all?
Is she short or is she tall?
Why does she make other girls cry?

Kara opened her eyes. Randi turned on her flashlight again. The girls lay in their sleeping bags, staring, wide-eyed in the dim light.

"I thought you turned it off," Robyn said.

Kara looked at the karaoke machine. The lights were on again.

"I did," said Kara.

"You're playing tricks," said Robyn.

"No, I'm not," said Kara.

"Turn it off," said Robyn.

"And this time pull out the plug," added Jill.

Kara got up and did that. Then she got back into her sleeping bag. She had a feeling that someone was playing tricks. But it wasn't her.

Soon the girls were all asleep again. But not for long.

Why does she make other girls cry?
Why does she hurt and why does she lie?

Kara woke up again. She felt groggy.

"What's going on?" Jill asked. She sounded wide-awake and frightened.

Robyn took the flashlight from Randi. She shined it at Kara. "Why didn't you turn it off?" Robyn asked angrily.

The light hurt Kara's eyes. She used her hand to block it. "I did," she said.

"Then why does it keep going back on?" asked Jill.

"You're trying to scare us," Robyn said.

"No, I'm not," said Kara. "I don't know why it keeps going on."

Kara knew her friends wanted her to get out of her sleeping bag and turn off the machine. She just wanted to pull a pillow over her head and go back to sleep. But she dragged herself out of the bag and went to the machine. In the dim glow of Randi's flashlight, she could see that the electric cord was no longer plugged into the wall.

"It's not plugged in," she said.

For a moment, the other girls were silent.

"Does it have batteries?" asked Randi.

"That must be it," Kara said. She looked behind the machine. Sure enough, there was a place for batteries. Kara took out the batteries. The karaoke machine stopped playing and went dark.

Kara sighed with relief and crawled back into her sleeping bag. All she wanted to do was close her eyes and sleep.

Who's the meanest girl of all?
Is she short or is she tall?

Why does she make other girls cry?
Why does she hurt and why does she lie?

The karaoke machine had started playing again.

"What's going on?" Jill gasped in the dark. She sounded like she was going to cry.

Robyn turned on the flashlight. Once again she aimed it at Kara. "I thought you unplugged it and took the batteries out," Robyn said angrily.

"I did," said Kara. She sat up in her sleeping bag. The red and white lights on the karaoke machine glowed. She didn't understand how that was possible.

"I'm tired of your tricks," Robyn said.

"I'm not playing tricks," said Kara.

"I don't believe you," Robyn said.

"Then go see for yourself," said Kara.

Robyn got out of her sleeping bag. She shined the flashlight on the machine. The cord was unplugged and the batteries were out. She pressed the OFF button. The machine kept playing. She turned down the volume. The mean girl song kept going.

"I don't get it," Robyn said.

Kara got out of her sleeping bag. She joined Robyn next to the machine.

"Why does it keep playing that song?" Jill asked.

Robyn made a fist and banged the top of the machine.

Who's the meanest girl of all?
Is she short or is she tall?
Why does she make other girls cry?
Why does she hurt and why does she lie?
What did Dana Merrill ever do to you?

Kara caught her breath and took a step back.

"Oh, my gosh!" Jill cried.

"Why did it say that?" Randi asked.

Kara wondered if Dana had planned this. Did Dana suspect Kara and her friends would be nasty? Did she program the machine to do this if they were mean to her?

What did Dana Merrill ever do to you?

"Make it stop!" Jill gasped.

Thump! Robyn pushed over the machine.

But the machine's lights still glowed. Robyn and Kara bent over the karaoke machine. Robyn shined the flashlight on it and searched for a way to turn it off. Randi got out of her sleeping bag and joined them.

What did Dana Merrill ever do to you?

"It won't turn off," said Randi.

"I want to go home!" Jill cried. She crawled out of her sleeping bag and hurried up the basement stairs.

"Me, too." Randi took the flashlight from Robyn and went up the stairs. Now Kara and Robyn were left in the dark.

What did Dana Merrill ever do to you?

A chill ran up Kara's spine. From the top of the stairs came the sound of a doorknob rattling.

"It's locked!" Jill gasped.

"There's no lock," said Kara. "The door must be stuck."

More rattling sounds came from the top of the stairs.

"It won't open!" Jill cried.

Kara went up the stairs and tried the door. The knob turned, but the door wouldn't open.

"There must be a light," Jill said.

Of course! Kara had forgotten. In the dark, she felt for the light switch and turned it on.

The basement stayed dark. Kara tried the switch again and again.

"The lights won't go on!" Jill wailed.

Kara tried the door again. She pulled as hard as she could, but it wouldn't open.

What did Dana Merrill ever do to you?

The song played over and over. The girls grew more and more frightened.

Kara banged her fists against the basement door. "Mom? Dad?"

"Help!" Jill shouted.

What did Dana Merrill ever do to you?

"Make it stop!" Jill cried.

Randi shined the flashlight back down into the basement. The beam swept past the couch. It stopped on the sports equipment in the corner.

"The bat," said Randi.

Robyn crossed the basement and got the bat. She went back to the karaoke machine.

What did Dana —

Crash! Robyn swung the bat down as hard as she could. The machine stopped playing. At the top of the basement stairs, Kara felt a wave of relief. She tried the doorknob again, but it spun loosely in her hand.

Who's the meanest girl of all?
Is she short or is she tall?

Kara and the other girls twisted their heads. The karaoke machine was lying on the basement floor.

The lights once again glowed, and the sound was as loud as ever.

Crash! Crash! Robyn swung the bat down. She hit the machine again and again. Glass shattered. Pieces of broken plastic banged off the wall.

Why does she make other girls cry?
Why does she hurt and why does she lie?

Crash! Crash! Robyn swung again and again. The broken thing on the floor no longer looked like a karaoke machine. It was just battered, dented pieces.

What did Dana Merrill ever do to you?

"It's haunted!" Randi gasped.

Robyn dropped the bat and ran up the stairs two steps at a time. She pushed past the other girls and banged on the door, screaming, "Help!"

Who's the meanest girl of all?
Is she short or is she tall?

The basement was dark. The batteries in Randi's flashlight had run out. The four girls huddled together at the top of the stairs. They clung to one another and sobbed in fear. Their faces were streaked with tears. Their throats were sore from screaming. Their hands hurt from banging on the basement door.

What did Dana Merrill ever do to you?

Stop! Kara thought miserably. *Please stop!*

Who's the meanest girl of all?

I promise I'll never be mean again, she thought. *Just please stop!*

The doorknob turned and the door opened. The sudden light blinded the girls. Wailing and sobbing, they stumbled into the kitchen, crying for their mothers.

"What on earth happened?" Mrs. Green asked.

The girls' mothers came and took them home. Mrs. Green calmed Kara down. She showed Kara that the basement door worked fine. As soon as you turned the knob, the door opened. The basement light worked, too. Mrs. Green went downstairs to the basement. When she saw the broken karaoke machine, she became upset. Now she would have to buy the Merrills a new one. On the floor she found the CD for the machine. Kara told her to play it so she would hear the song that scared the girls so much.

Mrs. Green played the whole CD.

Twice.

There was no such song.

The Nicest
Babysitter in the World

"Kids, this is Tanya," said Mrs. McPhee. "She'll be your babysitter tonight."

Tanya had long black hair and a warm smile. "Hi, kids. We're going to have a lot of fun."

Derek and Sarah McPhee stared uncertainly at the teenager. She looked and sounded nice, but she was new. And they were always nervous when a new babysitter came.

"You don't have to worry," said Mrs. McPhee.

"Tanya sat for the Smiths last week. Mrs. Smith says she's the nicest babysitter ever."

The McPhees asked Tanya to make sure Derek and Sarah had a good, healthy dinner that night. Mrs. McPhee said the children were only allowed to watch one hour of TV. Then they went out.

"So what would you like to do first?" asked Tanya after Mr. and Mrs. McPhee left.

"Play Candy Land," said Sarah.

"I love that game," said Tanya.

They played Candy Land. Derek thought Tanya was lots of fun. But once when Derek looked at her, Tanya looked old. Her skin looked wrinkled, her nose hooked, and a hairy mole grew from her chin. Derek rubbed his eyes, and Tanya looked like a teenager again.

"It's time for dinner," Tanya said when they finished playing Candy Land. "What would you like to eat?"

Derek and Sarah knew they were supposed to have a "good, healthy dinner." But those dinners were always boring.

"I wish we could have ice cream and cookies," said Sarah.

"Good idea," said Tanya.

Derek and Sarah stared at each other in surprise.

After a dinner of ice cream and cookies, Tanya said. "What do you want to do now?"

"Can we watch TV?" asked Derek.

"Sure," said the babysitter.

After they'd watched TV for an hour, the McPhee kids looked at Tanya. "Do we have to turn it off?" asked Derek.

Tanya shook her head. "You can watch as much as you like."

Derek and Sarah grinned. Their mother was right. Tanya was the nicest babysitter in the world!

The McPhee kids watched all their favorite shows. After a while Tanya said, "Is there anyone in the neighborhood you don't like?"

"Why do you want to know?" asked Derek.

"Oh, I don't know," said Tanya. "It just seems like everyone has someone they don't like." Then she smiled. For a second, it looked to Sarah like some of Tanya's teeth were missing. The other teeth looked crooked and yellow. Sarah blinked. When she looked again, all of Tanya's teeth were straight and white.

"Mom says we're not supposed to say bad things about people," said Sarah.

"I know," said Tanya. "And you're not supposed to have cookies and ice cream for dinner. And you're not supposed to watch all the TV you want. But isn't it fun?"

Derek and Sarah nodded.

"Talking about people you don't like is fun, too," said Tanya.

Derek wasn't sure. But Tanya seemed so nice, and they were having lots of fun. So maybe she was right.

"There's a boy down the street named Billy Thomas," Derek said. "Sometimes he throws rocks at us."

"Really?" Tanya said.

"Yes," said Sarah. "And he once kicked our dog. And another time, he pushed over my bike and broke one of the pedals."

"That's not nice," said Tanya.

"And he says bad things, too," said Derek.

"That's terrible," said Tanya. "If you could get back at him, what would you do?"

Derek and Sarah shared a look. It was as if Tanya had read their minds. They'd always wanted to get back at Billy.

"I'd push *his* bike down," said Sarah.

"Not me," said Derek. "I'd hit him as hard as I could on the arm."

"I'd throw a rock at him," said Sarah.

"Me, too," said Derek.

"And it would feel good, right?" Tanya said. "After all the mean things he's done to you."

Derek nodded. It would feel good. But thinking about it made him feel bad. "Our parents say it's wrong to hurt people."

"Does Billy Thomas think it's wrong?" Tanya asked.

Derek and Sarah shook their heads.

"Then maybe sometimes it's wrong," said Tanya. "But sometimes it's not."

Tanya let them stay up past their bedtimes. When it was finally time to go to bed, she said they didn't have to brush their teeth. Tanya tucked Sarah into bed and then came into Derek's room. She sat on the edge of Derek's bed.

"Did you have fun tonight?" she asked.

Derek nodded. "I wish you could always be our babysitter."

"I wish I could, too," said Tanya. "But I have to go away tomorrow, and I don't know when I'll be back."

Derek frowned.

Tanya reached into her pocket. "Would you like to have a picture to remember me?"

"Yes," said Derek.

Tanya gave him a picture of herself. Derek put it on the night table beside his bed.

The next morning, Mr. and Mrs. McPhee couldn't understand why their children slept so late. Mrs. McPhee called them for breakfast. Derek and Sarah came down and sat at the kitchen table. Derek felt groggy and slow. Sarah had a stomachache.

The McPhee children didn't touch the pancakes their mother had made. Derek had no appetite. He wished he could put his head down on the table and go back to sleep. Sarah looked pale and sat with her arms folded across her stomach.

"What's wrong?" Mrs. McPhee asked. "Why aren't you hungry?"

Derek and Sarah didn't answer.

"Did something happen last night?" Mrs. McPhee asked.

Derek and Sarah shared a look. They both shook their heads. They didn't want to tell on Tanya.

"I don't understand why you're acting like this," said Mrs. McPhee. "Tanya said you were both perfect angels."

Derek slid down in his chair. He had not been a perfect angel. He'd broken the rules last night. It was fun to do the things he wasn't supposed to do. But this morning, he felt bad. Maybe it wasn't always good to get what you wished for.

The phone rang and Mrs. McPhee answered it. "Hello? Oh, hi, Linda. What? Oh, that's terrible!"

Mrs. McPhee looked very upset. She hung up the phone and shook her head sadly.

"What's wrong, Mom?" Derek asked.

"That was Billy's mother," Mrs. McPhee said. "The most terrible thing happened. Billy got up early this morning and went for a bike ride."

Sarah and Derek shared a nervous look.

"Did someone push him off his bike?" Sarah asked.

"No," said Mrs. McPhee. "It's even worse. Someone threw a rock at him. He fell off his bike and knocked out both front teeth."

Sarah and Derek stared at each other with wide eyes. But neither said a word.

Later in the morning, Derek went back to his room. He tried to play with his Legos, but he couldn't stop thinking about the night before. Both he and Sarah had said they wanted to throw a rock at Billy.

Then Derek remembered the picture on his night table. He got up to look at it. In the picture, Tanya smiled at him with her straight white teeth. But in his hand, the picture began to change. Tanya's nose grew long and hooked. Her skin became wrinkled, and a hairy mole grew from her chin. Her teeth became crooked and yellow.

The next thing Derek knew, he was staring at a witch.